TWO

BUMS

BY

RUSSELL MCKENNETH

This story is dedicated to my Dad, Ken McBride

Thanks, Dad, for giving me the greatest gift of all,

A warped sense of humour.

CHAPTER 1

It was a beautiful spring morning. The sun had just popped its' warm, friendly face over the horizon and was glistening off of the dew that had settled on the guano that covered the dock. A flock of seagulls were squabbling over some bait that was left over from the previous night's fishermen. A small dog, wandering along the wharf-side, stopped to sniff some old rags that were piled up against the wall of the old, abandoned wool store. He snorted, lifted his leg in respect, and trotted off on his journey.

BAAAAAAAAAAAARP!

The horn of a ship that had been docked overnight, let loose on the silence. The small dog took off with its tail between its' legs, leaving a trail that the sun would clean up for it. The rag-pile came to life, screaming. Two hobos emerged like cartoon characters, running in mid-air.

"AHHHH!"! They screamed in unison.

"What the fffffff? Who the ffffff? Why the fffffff? AAHHHH?? Gasped the scruffy looking one.

"Oh my… Good Lord." Said the other scruffy looking one. "I don't think I'll ever get use to waking up like that." He started to settle down a bit. "Whew. That's enough to give a man a heart attack."

"It's enough to drive a man to drink, is what it is, Derrick." Said the first.

"Drive you to drink? What do you mean 'drive you to drink'? You don't need driven, Eric. You, my friend, are the chauffer!"

"That's a bit harsh." Said Eric, feigning offence "I can't help it if I get thirsty, now, can I?"

"Thirsty? Thirsty? A fish could not be so thirsty! In fact, do you know the worm at the bottom of a tequila bottle?"

"Www. er, yeah, I guess so…quite a few of them, I suppose. Why?" Eric said, not really sure of where this was going.

"Well let's just say, you'll never get worms," Derrick said.

"Funny Derrick. Very funny." Eric patted himself down and reached into the pocket inside his jacket, producing a well-used and battered, metal flask. "Speaking of which, would you like a drink?" Derricks mouth started watering in a Pavlovian manner.

"I wouldn't say no."

"I never thought for a second that you would" Eric said, handing the flask over to his friend. Derrick took it and held it up to the light. Not a particularly effective method of checking the contents of a metal container, but it was the one he chose.

"Beautiful clarity."

"Ah, but of course" Said Eric "As you would expect." Derrick carefully removed the lid, put it up to his nose and quickly jerked his head away like it was smelling salts.

"And a bouquet like a baboons' backside"

"Well, it could do with a bit of maturing."

"Ok. Well, here goes." Said Derrick as he took a swig. He handed the flask back to Eric and as he did so, his face turned a nasty, ashen, grey colour. Then red. Then, "Oooh (cough, cough), that's smooth. (Cough, cough, cough). Like a papercut." Eric eyed him up and down and then the much-used flask.

"Yeah. I wasn't sure if I should try it myself, but hey, you're still alive so… in for a penny…" Eric took a big gulp of the offending liquid.

Now, you know the silence that you get immediately after an explosive's tech pushes the plunger to detonate dynamite? Well, that is what Eric experienced next. Quickly followed by a brief inability to breathe, followed by a violent coughing fit. "Yeah, you're right." He squeaked.

"What vintage is this stuff, anyway" Derrick asked. He took back the container and peered into the hole as if looking for clues.

"Hmm. Not sure if it actually had a year," answered Eric, "but I'm sure it had a great night though." Eric looked back at the spot where he had been sleeping. Stretched, scratched himself, shook his head and added, "I don't suppose there's much point in going back to bed, now is there?"

"Not if you pressed the snooze button, there isn't, no. I don't want to go through that again in a hurry."

"Well, if that's a good nights' sleep, then I guess we've had it. I'm off to check out the water." And with that, he wandered off to the water's edge, pulling down his fly as he went.

"Oi, Eric! You can't do that there."

"Why not?"

"The people?" Derrick pointed at the ocean liner that was pulling out from the dock. "In the boat? They don't want the first thing that they see on their cruise to be you, having a slash, now do they?"

"Oh, I don't know. New York has its' Statue of Liberty. Sydney has its' Opera House and Bridge. Willington can have me, BLANK in hand, saluting as they sail merrily past."

"Or…" Said Derrick with an extended, theatrical pause, "Not!"

"Ok, I guess not then. I'll use the ramp." And, being a man of his word, he did. The ramp was only about 5 metres away. Eric went down the steps to the ramp, his voice drifting up with the sound of running… er… water. "Ahh. That's better."

"Oh great. A running commentary." Derrick mumbled under his breath. The sound of teeth being brushed soon drifted up after it. "Oh no, Eric! What on earth do you think that you're doing? You can't brush your teeth in that water. You've just peed in it." Eric came up the stairs wiping his mouth and adjusting himself.

"I was only brushing the ones I want to keep. And besides, what difference does a little pee make? Fish have been piddling in it since the dawn of time. It never hurt them. Why do you think the waters so salty?"

He stopped at the top of the stairs and looked out over the marina. "Wow. Would you take a look at that view. How lucky are we? I always wanted to have a harbour view, overlooking the marina. How peaceful. How serene."

"Apart from the alarm clock, you mean?" Said Derrick.

"Er… yeah. Apart from the alarm clock." Eric rubbed his hands over his face and brushed some of the drying salt water from his stubble. "Man, I thought I told you only to set that thing for workdays."

"Oh, I'm so sorry Eric." Derrick mocked. "I will try to remember that for tomorrow."

"You're forgiven. I know that you're only new to the job." He said. "Hey I'm starving. What's for breakfast?"

"Well, my good friend, I was thinking of something a bit foreign" Derrick started packing up all of his possessions, consisting of a backpack which doubled as a pillow and also a spare room.

"Foreign? Like that Scottish American place, McThingies? That's international at least."

"Oh, no, no, no, no." Said Derrick with a terrible French accent. "I saw ze French restaurant just along ze way yesterday. I am sure they will do a magnifique breakfast banquet."

"Buffet style, I hope. Either way, it sounds good to me. Some nice croissants would go down well about now." Eric picked up his bag and gestured to Derrick, "Lead the way, my friend, lead the way."

CHAPTER 2

An interesting thing about a town the size of Willington, is that you get good parts of town and the not-so-good parts of town. The good parts of town are generally safe to walk through any time of the day or night. The not-so-good parts… not-so-much.

It was in one of these 'good' parts of town, a few days earlier, that a young man, late teens, wearing what appeared to be a much bigger mans trousers and a set of headphones that seemed larger than his head, was walking by himself, contemplating the meaning of life and the universe. (Well, probably not. We all know that it's 42 anyway. But he certainly wasn't expecting what was about to transpire). Two men, dressed as clowns, stepped out from behind a bush, giving him such a start that it shocked him right out of his own little world.

"Boo." Said Charlie, the shorter of the two. "Ha, ha. Well, if it isn't young Mr. Alvin Spooner. Ha ha."

"Yeah, Spooner. Ha ha." Echoed the taller clown, Bozo. Like most clowns, Bozo, just for a bit of a giggle, was carrying a hessian sack concealing a sawn-off baseball bat.

"Blank off you freaks." Said Alvin with the eloquence that befitted his privileged up-bringing.

"Now that's not very nice Mr. Spooner." Said the spokesman. "You should be more politer to people what you doesn't know."

"Yeah. People what you doesn't know." Said Bozo.

"Yeah?" Alvin looked from one clown to the other and puffed his chest up. (Not much, mind, but you can only work with what you have), meanwhile, casting his mind back to what was behind him to see if a strategic retreat was a possibility. He couldn't see what Bozo had wrapped in his sack, but he knew that smacking balloon animals into the palm of your hand is nowhere near as intimidating as that. 'Bravado', he thought to himself. 'If I have enough bravado, I might just be able to make it to the corner behind them.' "Well, I think that you two should just Blank off and leave me alone." He tried to push past them, but Charlie put his hand on Alvins' shoulder with a lot more speed and force than Alvin was expecting.

"Wassa matter little boy?" Charlie said. "You don't like clowns?"

"Don't like clowns?" Bozo said.

"No. I don't like Blanking clowns." Alvin stepped into the smaller clown and chest-bumped him. He was now standing nose to rubber nose with him and although Alvin was about two inches taller than Charlie, the clown had him on a pound for pound basis, by about 130 Kilograms. 120 of which was standing behind him at that point. Being that all Alvin had in his toolbelt at this time was bravado, he added "I think all clowns should Blank off. Especially you two blanks."

"Nah. You don't mean that." Said Charlie, grabbing the sack off the big guy. "In fact, I think that you wants to run away to the circus." Bozo wrapped his big, meaty arms around the youth.

"Yeah, he he." Said Bozo as Charlie shoved the sack over Alvin's' head. "Fink you run away from the circus." Thinking and breathing can be considered multi-tasking for some people. Bozo doesn't multi-task.

"What the Blank do you think you're doing?" came a muffled voice from under the sack. "Blank off you Blanks." Charlie tied the binding from the bag around the hands of young Alvin.

"We can do this the easy way or hard way. The hard way involves pain. It's your choice."

"I like the hard way," said Bozo.

"Blank, Blank." Muffled Alvin, kicking out in the hope of making contact.

Charlie nodded his head at Bozo.

Bozo nodded his head back at Charlie and brought the cosh down on the back of Alvin's head.

Alvin nodded his head and then went limp. Bozo caught him before he hit the ground and threw him over his shoulder like a sack of potatoes.

"Quick Bozo. Get him in the van before anyone sees us." Said Charlie as he clicked the vans remote control and ran to the drivers' door. Bozo opened the rear door of the van and threw the boy onto the floor. "Careful with him Bozo. You don't want to hurt him. He's our meal ticket."

"But I just hit him over the head wiv a baseball bat."

"I know. I mean, we don't want to hurt him any more than we have to. We may have to get him to speak to his old man. You know, to prove that we have him."

"But if he doesn't come home for tea tonight, won't Mr. Spooner know that he's gone?" Said Bozo in a moment of clarity.

"Look… just get in the car." With that Charlie started the engine. Bozo slammed the back door shut and jumped into the passengers' seat. Charlie took off just as Bozo had almost gotten his door shut. "Good job it's a quiet street."

"Yeah. I don't like too much noise." Charlie didn't even look at him. He just drove.

The white van pulled up outside a huge roller-door. Attached to the roller-door, around the outside edges, was a large, abandoned warehouse. The area had been used as a logging yard and hence, was in the middle of a burned-out pine forest. A perfect location to hide someone that may have a tendency to call for help or scream from pain as their arms were being torn off. Out of the van jumped an oversized clown with bright red hair and a painted-on smile to match. He wrestled with a key for a few moments and eventually opened the small door next to the roller-door and went inside. There was a lot of noise and the sound of grunting, and the roller-door slowly raised to about five feet before it seized. Bozo ducked under it and came back outside. He walked around to the back of the van and went to open the back door. The door flew open with such force that it knocked Bozo clean off his feet. Alvin, still with his hands tied, had managed to wriggle the sack up just high enough so as he had a peep hole. He dived out of the van at full speed. The nature of the fabric of life, and indeed hessian, meant that the bag slipped back over his head and Alvin, all 5'6 of him, ran straight into the half-open roller-door, knocking him out cold again. Charlie got out of the driver's seat and walked around the back of the van to see Alvin lying unconscious on the ground and Bozo sitting, stunned, about 10 feet away, scratching his head.

"Well, don't just sit there Bozo, help our guest inside." Charlie ducked under the door. "Oh, and mind your head. That could give you a nasty bump."

CHAPTER 3

Eric and Derrick approached a strip of shops, one of which had a sign out the front which read 'Le RESTAURANT AU BORD DE LA MER" Underneath, in English for those of us with only half a brain, (French Cuisine).

"Here we are Eric, as promised, foreign food."

"Hmm. They appear to be closed at the moment. I assume that means that we use the tradesman's entrance?"

"Tradesman's entrance? My foot! We shall slip in the back way like all VIP's." Derrick tried the gate which was locked. "Would you like a leg-up?"

"Certainly. Thank you." Derrick cupped his hands and Eric put his foot in and stepped up and over. "Now I see why you're called Derrick. You lifted me with such ease."

"Ah. Yes. Humour. I remember that. I do believe it's supposed to happen after breakfast." Derrick looked left and right before hoisting himself over the fence. Before them, stood a large dumpster and several wheelie bins.

"I am so hungry," said Eric, "I could eat a scabby cat."

"You may just get your chance yet Eric. There's a few to choose from."

"I'll check out the buffet first if you don't mind. What did you say this place was called again?"

"Le Restaurant Le Merde." He replied. "Where you can have anything you like… as long as it's yesterdays."

Eric wandered over towards the bins and saw a large pile of wine bottles.

"Choice! Decisions, decisions. Ooh and look, the bar is open too."

"I wonder what we have today." Said Derrick as he rummaged through one of the bins. "Eww, that looks nasty." He dipped a piece of bread into something and put it up to his nose.

"Yeah, it does." Said Eric, distracted slightly from his flask. "What is it?"

"I'm not quite sure, but I think that cat over there just rejected it." He dropped the bread back in the bin.

"Violently too, by the looks of it. Now there's a problem that you don't get at the Red Dragon."

"No, True." Chuckled Derrick. "At the Red Dragon the cat is the slimy muck that gets put in the bin. If they don't re-hash it, that is."

"Drink, Derrick?" Said Eric, offering his now full flask to his test-pilot.

"Can I trust it?" He asked, pointing it away from himself as he unscrewed the lid. He took a sniff and looked at the beaten object. "Hey. It says here 'NOT TO BE CONSUMED'…oh…' ON AN EMPTY STOMACH'. I get it."

"Why? Does it give you hallucinations? There is no writing on that flask. With some of the stuff that I've put into it, it's a miracle that there's any flask left on that flask."

"Well. The proof is certainly in the drinking." Derrick cautiously took a swig and shuddered. "Yeesh… er… Hey, that's strangely moorish." He passed the canteen back to Eric, who also took a draft and started taking food out of various bins which he piled onto a discarded lid.

"Oh look. I didn't know that the French ate rice."

"I didn't know that rice wriggled."

"Oh well, it's all protein." Eric observed.

"Yes. If only those body builders knew what was in those expensive protein shakes, I'm sure that they wouldn't be quite so keen."

"Yep, and here we have it all laid on for us. What a life!"

CHAPTER 4

"What're we going to do with him now Charlie?" Asked Bozo. Alvin was sitting slumped, unconscious tied to a dining chair, sitting at a small table with a single light bulb hanging overhead by a piece of string. It wasn't lit of course, seeing as string isn't renowned for its' conductive properties, but it wasn't a bad effect if you like that sort of thing.

"No names Bozo, you idiot. We can't afford for him to know our identities."

"Sorry Charlie… Oops. I did it again, didn't I?"

"Hmmph. What d'you think?" Charlie slapped himself in the forehead, smudging his makeup. He looked at the palm of his hand and said, "Leave the bag on his head too Bozo. At least he can't finger our faces."

"Eww. That sounds disgusting."

"What does?"

"Having someone finger your face."

"You really are a bozo, aren't you Bozo?" Charlie grabbed a cloth and started to remove his clown makeup.

"Well? What're we going to do wiv him?"

"Look. I've been through this already. We ring his old man and get him to pay the ransom to get his kid back."

"What if he doesn't have any money?"

"Old man Spooner is the richest man in town. Of course he has money."

"But what if he doesn't want to pay?"

"Then we wring Juniors' neck." Charlie slapped Alvin on the back of the neck and Alvin reacted with a muffled response.

"Mfrphmmmrr."

"What'd he say?"

"Mfrphmmmrr… I fink."

"No. I mean, what is he trying to say?" Bozo
leaned forward and pulled the sack off Alvin's
head. Charlie tried to stop him, but it was too late.

"What were you trying to say?" Bozos big clown
face, inches away from Alvin's.

"No, you idiot," protested Charlie. "What did I say
about leaving the bag on his head?"

"Oh, you mean about fingering faces an 'at?" He
got back into Alvin's' face again and with two
fingers of one hand, slapped Alvin on the cheek.
"Oh yeah. You keep your fingers to yourself, ok?"
Charlie looked at Alvin, then at Bozo, then back at
Alvin and said,

"Now why didn't I think of that? Looks like we're
going to have to kill him now, damn it."

"Why?" Said Alvin.

"Yeah, why?" Echoed Bozo.

"Because… He's seen our faces, and he knows my name. That's why."

"So? That's no reason to Blank kill me." An element of panic had crept into Alvin's voice. The Bravado had run away, leaving behind a scared fifteen-year-old boy.

"If we don't kill you, you'll tell the cops, and we'll go to prison. I don't want to go to prison. My old man is in prison, and I don't even visit him. That's how much I don't want to go to prison."

"But you don't like the old man, Charlie. That's why you don't visit him." Said Bozo, scratching his head.

"Yeah, you're right. So, I don't want to move back in with him, do I?" Bozo looked at Charlie with a confused look on his face. Not that that was unusual for Bozo, but this time he was lost for words. A most unusual occurrence. He decided to just nod and shake his head as he saw appropriate.

"That's just the point Charlie." Said Alvin. "Can I call you Charlie? Anyway. That's just the point, Charlie. I don't like my old man either."

"And?" Said Charlie.

"Yeah. And?" Said Bozo.

"And… I wouldn't lay down my life for him… If you know what I mean." Charlie nodded his head instinctively and then it was his turn to look confused.

"Er… What DO you mean?"

"Yeah, What DO you mean?" Said Bozo. His expression hadn't changed, he always looked somewhat confused.

I mean, I know how much money the old cheese has. I also know where he keeps it. I know the combination to his safe. I also know that he won't part with it to get me back. Oh, you can try, but it won't work. What I'm saying is, he hates my guts. The only thing he hates more than me is my mother. The only reason he took custody of me is to Blank her off and so as she won't get to see any Blank maintenance money." Charlie rubbed his chin with his fingers.

"So. Tell me why we shouldn't kill you?" Bozo opened his mouth to speak. Charlie glared at him and held up a finger as if to hush him. Bozo closed his mouth.

"Because the old man doesn't like to part with his precious money, I'm going to have to show you how to get your greedy hands on it. First up, how much do you want for me?" The two looked at each other, bewildered.

"$50,000"

"Fifty thousand Blank bucks? Are you Blank joking?" Alvin's' voice went up a couple of octaves. "That's pocket change for him, and an insult to me. If you want me to help you, I'll have to be worth $200 thou… at least!"

CHAPTER 5

"Derrick rose to his feet, brushed some crumbs from the front of his shirt, took off his jacket, carefully folded it and shoved it into his duffel bag. "Have you just about finished there Eric?" He said. Eric was emptying the dregs from some bottles that were stored neatly in a dumpster.

"Why, do you have an appointment to get to?" Eric didn't look around.

"No, not really, but I do believe that the chef has a thing about sharing his fare with non-paying customers, and he has access to big knives. I think it's about time we moved along."

"Oh well, fare's fair." Eric quipped. "I guess that we have to leave something for the cats." He picked up his bag and threw it over his shoulder.

He winced as a whiskey bottle, filled with who-knows-what, hit him in the back. He looked at Derrick as if to say 'oops', shrugged, smiled and said' "Hurry up then, I'm waiting for you." And then jumped the gate. Derrick shook his head and followed.

The two men walked for about ten minutes in silence when Eric said, "You're very somber today, Derrick. What's up?"

"Oh, nothing really. D'you know what the date is?"

"It's about the 20th, I'd guess. Why?"

"It's the 22nd, actually." Said Derrick. "It's my birthday."

"Your birthday? Well happy birthday Derrick. Where's the party?"

"Where's the present?" Derrick answered flatly.

"Ah. Well. About that… er. Can you wait until payday?" Eric patted himself down as if searching for a wallet.

"You don't have a payday."

"Ok, well, fair enough then. Let's just say, don't hold your breath. It's not good for old blokes."

"Enough of the 'old' if you don't mind." Derricks mind continued to wander, not hearing what Eric had to say.

"You know what they say. You're only as old as the woman you're feeling, eh?" Eric joked. "Which in your case would require an incredible memory. He, he, HEY, watch out!" Eric reached out and grabbed Derrick by the back of his shirt collar and dragged him back just as he was stepping out onto the road. A shiny, silver Rolls Royce cruised past, not slowing down at all and narrowly missing Derrick. "Be careful man. You could have been killed."

"There but for me go I." He stared off in the direction of the limousine.

"What?" Said Eric. "Where did that come from?"

"Oh. There for me go I." Said Derrick, snapping out of his daze. "It's a miss-quote from the 16th century evangelist, John Bradford. Meaning that if I'd lived the life that I could have, it would have been me driving that Roller."

"You want to run over some homeless dude?"

"Well, no. But I wouldn't be the homeless dude, had I followed my dreams."

"Then why didn't you follow your dreams then?" Derrick turned to look at Eric and said,

"I just told you… Me! Every time that I'd come up with an idea, or look like I was moving ahead, I'd shoot myself in the foot. So here I am, living the good life." He put his hand on Erics' shoulder. "To tell you the truth Eric, if it wasn't for your friendship, I'd have stepped out in front of that car on purpose. Here I am. Another year older and nothing to show for it."

"Hey, look on the bright side. At least you don't have debt."

"Ha! That's what I like about you Eric, you always see the silver lining in every cloud."

"Er, I think it was a Silver Cloud, actually Derrick. The lining is usually leather." Eric said, trying to snap his friend out of his fug.

"Huh? Oh, of course. Ha. He did seem to be in a bit of a hurry. He didn't even slow down to see if we were ok."

"That was Spooner." Said Eric. "He wouldn't have even seen the likes of us, let alone care if we were alright."

"Well, I might have nothing, but at least I'm not like that. Money wouldn't stop me from caring about my fellow man."

"Like you say Derrick. That's why we're living the good life. Come on, let's go to the park. I'll shout you a birthday drink." Eric tapped the pocket where he kept the flask. Derrick shuddered and started salivating.

Eric and Derrick continued for a while each in their own thoughts, when Derrick broke the silence. "So, who is this Spooner guy, anyway? I see his name around the place all the time, but I really don't know much about him."

"Spooner? He's the richest man in town." Eric answered. "Not exactly who you'd call Mr. Nice Guy either. A real nasty piece of work, actually. He used to own the old timber mill until it, ahem, burned down. He is also the main reason why there is such a high unemployment rate in town. It used to be said that more than half Willington's' population was employed by the mill, either directly, or indirectly. After the fire there were no jobs left. Spooner sourced the timber from overseas somewhere at a lower cost and quality, then on-sold it at higher prices and even higher profits. Not that I think that making a profit is a crime, but with him, the profit was more important than anything else. Even his own son can't stand him apparently."

"I knew that I'd heard the name before. There was a lad named Spooner at the school when I was teaching there, but he wouldn't let anyone call him that." Said Derrick. "Alan? Alwin? Something like that, anyway. Tough little blighter. And smart, too. But always getting into trouble. He wasn't in my class, but I recall some of the other teachers talking about him. Saying something about his father not wanting to spend the money on a private school education for him."

"Yep. That sounds like him. From what I hear, the boy is a real rebel that wants to undo everything that his old man has ever done. Like I said, Spooner is a nasty piece of work." Eric mulled the conversation over in his mind as they walked along the footpath and then added,

"Some say that Spooner is totally ruthless.

Some say that Spooner had the fire lit himself.

Some say that the insurance payment was extremely high.

Some say that he paid off the police so as he didn't go down for it.

Some say that a lot of important papers were destroyed in the fire.

Some say that there's a lot of truth in what 'some say'."

CHAPTER 6

"Why won't you let me call him?" Said Bozo in a deep, but somehow, whiney voice.

"Because, my little brother, I can speak in complete sentences."

"Me too."

"Ok then," said Charlie, "I can walk and chew gum at the same time and I don't consider it 'Multi-tasking'." Bozo thought about this for a moment.

"Fair enough then. You win."

"Ok Einstein," Alvin butted in. "Do you know what you're going to say to him when he answers the phone?"

"Of course, but if I get into trouble, you be ready to scream, ok?"

"Blank yeah." Alvin punched his fist into his hand. "I've been waiting for the opportunity to get back at the old Blank for years."

"Sounds good enough for me." Said Charlie, handing an old burner phone to Alvin. "You dial the number and I'll speak to him."

Alvin put the phone on loudspeaker and punched in the numbers. It took a few seconds before the ring tone started and he passed the phone back to Charlie.

"Spooner!" Said a gruff voice on the other end of the line. Alvin nodded at Charlie for identification.

"Mr. Spooner?" Charlie's voice exuded confidence.

"Yes. Who is this?" Spooner's voice exuded abruptness and impatience.

"It doesn't matter who this is. What matters is what I have to say." Said Charlie, cool calm and collected.

"Then say then and Blank off. I'm a busy man." His voice was not cool, calm or collected. It was more like, short, sharp and to the point.

"We have your son, Alvin."

"Good. Send him home when you're done with him." The phone went dead.

"Hello? Hello?" Charlie looked over at Alvin. "You're right. He doesn't like you."

"I thought you meant that I was right, he's a Blank hole. Quick. Call him back!" Alvin rose to his feet with his fists, knuckles down, on the table. "He's Blanking with your head. And be forceful. Don't Blank around. Remember, you are in charge." Alvin quickly punches the number back into the phone and slides it across the table to Charlie.

"Spooner."

"Now listen here Blank and listen good. That little hang-up just cost you big time. I was going to ask you for two hundred thousand, but it just went up to half a Mill. If I don't get the money by tomorrow it will cost your son a digit, and you another hundred K. Every day you Blank around, it'll cost you. The less there is of him, the more it'll cost to get him back. Do-you-get-my-meaning?"

"You're bluffing."

"Ya think so?" Charlie points to Alvin who cracks his knuckles and screams.

"Ahh! Blank. Me Blanking fingers!" Charlie put the phone back to his mouth.

"I'll send the first finger to you. The next one goes to the newspapers. Oh, and no. I'm not bluffing. I'll call you back with some drop off details." Charlie pushed the hang up button.

"Blank." Said Spooner as the phone went dead.

"That was impressive." Said Alvin, as Charlie breathed a big sigh of relief. "Do you have a manager?"

"I can handle myself, thanks all the same."

"Yeah. Mum's always telling him off for it." Said Bozo, dead pan.

"Well leave it alone until we get the money." Responded Alvin. "We've got work to do."

"What're you mean, 'When WE get the money'? This is me an' Bozo's scam. You're just a prisoner."

"Yeah. Just a prisoner."

"Which is exactly what you two Blanks will be if I don't help you." Said Alvin, looking from one to another. "Cut me in, or I don't tell you the next step.

"It was his idea to ask for half a million instead of fifty thousand, Charlie. That's ten percent more than we would'a got."

"Math's was never his strong subject." Said Charlie.

"What was? Beating up little kids for their lunch money?"

"Nah. The big kids were much more fun." Bozo laughed. "And they were too embarrassed to dob on me."

"They got more lunch money too." Charlie added. "You've gotta love a good win/win. Ok, you're in, but not a full cut. Twenty percent." Bozo started counting on his fingers with a blank expression on his face.

"Forty percent." Alvin bounced back.

"Twenty-five, and that's it."

"Ok. I can live with that." Alvin put his hand out and shook Charlies' hand.

"But Charlie. That's two and half million dollars!"

"He's good." Alvin said. "I wouldn't advise that you let him do your bookkeeping though."

"Yeah. I saw him with a book once'. Said Charlie, shaking his head. "He looked at it for about 30 seconds and then started chewing the corners. How quick do you reckon it'll take the old man to get the money together?"

"If I know him as well as I think I do, he'll have started calling in the money already."

"What do you mean by 'calling the money in?"

"He doesn't always keep it at home," said Alvin. "He loans it out to poor desperate suckers, that have to pay him back at usurious interest rates. He'll have Franko and the boys go 'round and collect. Franko loves his job. He can be very persuasive. I don't doubt that he'll get back a lot more than he ever loaned out."

"I read a book once." Bozo interrupted. "That one about the talking mouse and his doggie." Charlie and Alvin turned and looked at Bozo with their mouths open.

"Er. That was a Mickey Mouse comic, Bozo."

"'t's still a book." Bozo insisted.

"And a very cultural one at that, I'm sure." Said Charlie. "Now where were we?"

"We were about to work out a drop off point for me old man to leave the money."

"Leave the money? Aren't we going to meet in a dark alley and exchange briefcases, or something?"

"I don't think that that would be a good idea. For starters, dad won't be there, Franko and the boys will. Secondly, you'll never get out alive. Even

Bozo here would be no match for Franko and co."
Alvin rubbed his chin in a clique` kind of way,
"Hey, you guys are good at disguises, yeah? I've
got an idea."

CHAPTER 7

Back in Sir Reginald Spooners' office, Spooner was sitting at his desk going through some paperwork. He picked up the telephone and dialed out.

"Mr. Franko? I have a job for you." He said. "I need for you to make a few collections for me. Get around here straight away, would you. I'll have a shopping list waiting for you." He didn't wait for a reply before hanging up. About fifteen minutes later, the front doorbell rang. It was Franko. Not a particularly big man in all reality, but he seemed big. He had a bigness to him that would intimidate most.

"Let yourself in Mr. Franko. I'm in the study." Said a voice from a speaker next to the video camera, located by the doorframe, followed by a click. Franko let himself in and went through to the study.

"You called for me Mr. Spooner?"

"You're alone?" Said Spooner. "I expected you to have some helpers."

"I'll pick up Tommy on the way out to the job. What's happening?"

"Alvin, the little Blank, has gotten himself into some Blank again," said Spooner, handing a piece of paper to Franko. "Once again, I'm having to bail him out. I need you to recall some debts for me. Here's a list. I need five hundred 'G' by tomorrow morning." Franko looked down at the paper that Sir Reginald had passed to him and smiled.

"That's doable. I'll get Tommy. We're onto it straight away sir."

"That's what I like to hear. See you in the morning." Spooner went back to his paperwork. Without looking up he said, "You can let yourself out." Franko had already left the room.

CHAPTER 8

Eric and Derrick came to the park around late morning. As they walked under a cast iron archway with 'WILLINGTON BOTANICAL GARDENS' written across the top, they saw what appeared to be a body, presumed asleep, judging by the snoring noise coming from under the newspaper which covered their face.

"Heh heh. Looks like someone had a big night last night." Said Eric, giving Derrick a nudge.

"It does, doesn't it." Said Derrick. "Wait up." He was stopped by a headline of the paper. He carefully slipped the front page off and page 4, (it's always continued on page 4). He continued walking and reading. "My goodness. It says here that the mint is releasing $500 and $1000 notes as regular currency."

"Why on earth would they do a thing like that?"

"It says that it will make the smaller denominations last longer because they won't have to use as many."

"They won't have to use many on me, that's for sure." Said Eric. "I don't remember the last time I saw a 50."

"Too true. The average person will have to give change when they get their wages. How ripped off would you feel?"

"The way prices are going; it will cost that much just to pay attention."

"Good job you don't do it very often then, isn't it?"

"Sorry?" Said Eric. "What was that? My mind wandered then."

"As I said." They walked on and found a tree near a clearing and instinctively went over and sat down. Eric pulled the flask from his pocket.

"Happy birthday Derrick." He said. "Here's to you." He took a swig and handed it over to Derrick.

"Thank you." He said before taking a mouthful. "Funny thing about birthdays. They get you thinking about people and things that you've known and done. You were in real estate before you made the street change, weren't you?"

"Yes. I was good at it too."

"Then what happened? I thought realtors made a fortune."

"They do… In the good times. And, of course, if they're smart, they hang on to it in the bad times. I wasn't. Do you remember what I said about the Old Timber Mill?"

"What, about it being the main industry for the whole town?"

"Yeah. What do you think happens to a one-horse town when the horse dies?"

"No-one buys real estate, I guess." Said Derrick.

"Worse than that," Eric explained, "land values drop, half the people move out of town because they have no work and the mug that's over-extended himself to invest in rentals, is left with a whole heap of properties that are not worth anything. I walked away with nothing but the clothes on my back and a credit history that made sure that I wasn't getting any more. And do you know the real clincher? Guess who bought up all of the properties for next to nothing. Yep, you got it. The guy who burned down the mill. Spooner! Probably paid for it with the shipload he got from the insurance company."

"Wow. That is so cruel." Said Derrick. He drank some more and handed the flask back to Eric.

"The only good to come of it, I suppose, is that he also owns the dock that we sleep on at night and the park that we're sitting in. I heard that he leases the park back to the council, so as they can keep it free for the people. Otherwise, he'd build on it."

"I suppose he can't be all bad then. At least he lets the council lease the park. He could have built on it to increase his asset base."

"Except that there was no money left in town for him to reap from. If he can get paid for looking like the good guy, he can wait until land values go back up. Not stupid, is he."

"Cleverer than a lab-rat." Said Derrick, shaking his head.

"Enough about me, "Said Eric, changing the subject. "How did you wind up in this Grand old Manor with gutter glimpses?"

"You used to write your own copy, didn't you?"

"Absolutely." Said Eric. "You never trust the important things to anyone else."

"I wouldn't blame your downfall all on the economy, Eric. Sometimes you should leave poetic license to the poets… Just saying." Eric didn't respond to this slight. He just looked at Derrick until he continued. "Oh, me? As you know, I was a schoolteacher. I was transferred out here a couple of years ago. My wife… well, ex-wife now, came out here with me just long enough to help me to get established. Then one day I came home to and empty house. It turns out that she'd planned it all along. I thought that we were planning to start a family. In reality, she was. Just not with me. It really messed with my brain. I had an emotional break-down. Lost my job. Lost my house. Lost everything I had. I hate to admit it, but I cried for weeks. I couldn't teach school in that condition. The kids would have killed me, not to mention the teachers." Derrick cleared his throat. Eric passed him the communal flask which he accepted. "It taught me some serious lessons though. I discovered that life isn't about people or things, but about living. The streets gave me back my sanity, in a crazy sort of way."

"Do you miss that life at all?"

"The kids… I miss the kids I used to teach, but that's about it."

They both sat in silence for a while, thinking about the conversation that they had just had, wondering why they hadn't discussed their pasts much before. Eric looked at his empty, left wrist.

"Look at the time. We'd better be heading home, otherwise we won't get the good spot."

"Let's go past the '5 Day Café' on the way. They close just after lunch trade."

"But it's way past lun… Silly me, Of course." Said Eric, shaking his head. "best we get there before the vermin. I don't like bread with those black bits in them. Try telling me that they're wholegrains… Huh! Hey, we may be able to find you some birthday cake."

"Oh… Yummy…," said Derrick. "Stale cake… What more could a man ask for?"

CHAPTER 9

Back in the warehouse, Alvin, Charlie, and Bozo were standing around the table. In the middle of the table was a mobile phone, possibly the smartest thing in the room, with the exception of Alvin's' mouth, of course. Alvin started pacing, turned around and thumped the table with his fist.

"Ok. I think that we've let him stew for long enough. Give him a call and arrange for him to drop off the dough."

"Alright then. You know the number better than me." Said Charlie. "Dial away." Alvin picked up the phone, punched in the numbers and handed it back to Charlie.

"Spooner!" Snapped Spooner on the other end of the line.

"Mr. Spooner. Do you have the money, or do we have to start performing surgery?"

"Ow, ow." Cried Alvin. "Not the bolt cutters. Blank!"

"I have the money." Said Spooner, calm as a cucumber and very much in control. "Where do you live? I'll send my associates around and deliver it personally."

"That won't be necessary." Replied Charlie, equally as calm. "I want you to deliver it in person, to a trash can on the corner of Long and Hall streets. Do you know where that is? Of course you do. You own it. Put it in a plain, brown paper bag and drop it in the bin at exactly ten past nine AM in the morning. Then drive off. We will be watching you. No tricks. No Police. No bull Blank! Alright?"

"And what about the boy?"

"When we have the money and have counted it, we will drop him off unharmed. Provided it's all there. You break the rules, we break your son. Understand?"

"Oh, I understand alright." Said Spooner and slammed down the phone. There is something about slamming down a desk phone that is totally lost on a mobile. "Alvin is going to pay me back every cent of this. One way or another."

"That all seemed to go well." Said Charlie.

"Yes." Said Alvin. "Worrying, isn't it?"

"What d'you mean?"

"Yeah. What you mean?"

"He can't be trusted." Said Alvin. "He'll be up to something. He always is."

"It's ok. We'll have the area staked out long before he's even out of bed. I can smell a cop a mile off."

"Yeah. Smelly cop a mile off." Alvin and Charlie both looked at Bozo with a 'what are you on'? look on their faces and then back at each other.

"The cops are the least of our problems." Said Alvin. "Mr. Franko is the one that you should be concerned about. Cops have rules to follow. Mr. Franko makes his own rules. Then breaks them. He's one nasty piece of Blank. That's why he gets along with father so well. Neither of them have any morals."

"No problems." Reassured Charlie. "We have disguises." Alvin wasn't feeling all that reassured.

"I hope that they're more convincing than the ones you used to kidnap me."

"Oh, they are. Real convincing."

"Yeah. Real convvv… What he said."

CHAPTER 10

The next day was a day like any other day. It started with a beautiful red sunrise and ended in a 'y'. Eric and Derrick left the dock in the search of some relatively fresh food.

"Why don't we go back to the restaurant that we had breakfast at yesterday?" asked Eric.

"I'm not sure if they are open on Mondays."

"When is Monday?"

"Yesterday." Said Derrick. "If they weren't open yesterday, then the slops are going to be even sloppier."

"Oh yes. I remember the last time that happened." Said Eric, holding his stomach down low. "A most uncomfortable experience."

"Never mind. There are plenty of other places around."

"Let's make it somewhere that's licensed. I need a top up." Said Eric, tapping his breast pocket. "We cleaned me out last night, celebrating your birthday."

"Ok. I think I know just the spot." It wasn't far down the road before Derrick tested a gate. The gate opened with relative ease and no dogs barked, so Derrick went in closely followed by Eric.

"I remember this place. We haven't been here for ages."

"Yes. They've been renovating. They have only just reopened."

"How do you know all of this stuff?" asked Eric.

"I keep my eyes open while you have your head stuck in other people's wheelie-bins."

"You just never know what you'll get."

"Hmm. Dysentery? Salmonella? Botulism? Listeria?... Just to name a few possibilities."

"Yes, well. That's' life, living on the edge." Said Eric. "Where's breakfast? I'm starved."

"I'll check out the pantry." Said Derrick, heading towards a dumpster. "Oh no."

"What?"

"The bin is empty. They must have had a collection last night."

"At least the bottles are still there." Said Eric. He picked up one with a familiar label and put it to his nose. "Oh. Pffft." He said in disgust.

"What's wrong, has it gone sour?"

"Worse than that." Eric tipped the remaining contents onto the ground. "They've been washed. Who'd do a thing like that?"

"Well, I shan't be coming back here, I can assure you of that. Nor will I be recommending it to my friends."

"He, he… Friends!"

"Let's get out of here. There must be somewhere else."

"Sure. We'd better get a move on though. Staff are going to start turning up soon."

The two men headed off down the road, Eric, checking the various wheelie bins as they went, every now and then, finding something to snack on, but nothing very substantial. As they wandered towards the middle of town they saw two other bums, stood, leaning against a wall near a council bin. As they walked past them, Eric caught the eye of the shorter of the two.

"Hi." Said Eric as a friendly gesture. The bum said nothing. Just looked through him. Eric felt uncomfortable, so he didn't bother looking in that bin.

"Amateurs." Said Derrick after they were past.

"What do you mean?"

"Their shoes were too new, faces too clean. They're just homeless wannabes. One of them is even wearing a wristwatch."

"Why on earth would anyone 'wannabe' homeless?"

"Metro-homeless." Said Derrick. "They just want to 'look' homeless. It's a status thing."

"What. As in Bum is the new Black?"

"Something like that. If you identify as homeless, no-one expects to much from you." They rounded the corner and Eric spotted another wheelie bin and headed straight for it.

"It's true. No-one expects anything from me." He lifted the lid and saw a brown paper parcel which he lifted out.

"And you always deliver, my friend. You always deliver. Don't spoil your dinner now Eric."

"I won't mum. Promise." He opened the parcel and looked inside and closed it again quickly. Looked left and right, peered into the package again and shut it again, just as quickly. He clutched it close to his chest and hurried away.

"What's the matter?... Eric?? What's up?? Eric?"? Derrick hurried after his friend. "Eric? Talk to me… Eric?"

CHAPTER 11

Derrick finally caught up with Eric at the entrance to the park, although Eric hadn't slowed down the whole way. "What is the matter with you Eric?" He said. Eric looked around and made a beeline for the mensroom. "Are you ok? Are you sick or something?" Derrick was seriously starting to whine by this stage. As they entered the toilets, Eric grabbed Derrick by the lapels and dragged him into a cubicle. "Hey, don't be so rough." Eric shut the door behind them and made sure that it was locked.

"Take a look at this." Eric said as he shoved the parcel into Derricks hands. Derrick tentatively looked into the bag and slammed it shut again as if to stop the contents from escaping. He opened it up again and they both peered in and shut it again.

"Oh. My. Goodness! Do you know what this is?"

"I am afraid to even assume that I might even hazard a guess as to what this might be." They both look back into the bag at the bundles of $1000.00 notes.

"I never thought I'd see the day when I'd see anything that big, let alone hold it." Said Eric reaching into the bag and taking out a wad. "It feels so…" A few stalls down there was a flush. Eric and Derrick went silent, Eric shoving the notes back in the bag.

"Daddy, why are two men in the same room?" Said a small voice.

"I don't know sweetheart." Said a man's voice. "Maybe one of them is a doctor." He sounded unsure of himself, but an answer is an answer. "Just let's hurry along, alright."

"But I hasn't washeded my hands yet."

"It's ok sweetie. We'll wash them twice later." And they were gone.

"We'd better get the heck out of here." Said Derrick after a brief pause.

"Why? What's the rush?"

"I just re-wound in my head what we said and what they heard. If I was 'Daddy', I would have the cops down here quicker than you can say Jack Russell."

"Hmm. I hadn't thought of that." Derrick opened the door and peeked around the corner.

"The coast is clear."

"Ok." Said Eric. "You go ahead. I'll be with you in a minute."

"What're you doing?"

"Hey, when in Rome… and when a man's gotta go, a man's gotta go."

"Ok but hurry up." Said Derrick. "We have to get out of here quick-smart." Derrick went to the doorway and waited just out of view of anyone that may be watching. Eric, on the other hand, didn't have another hand, so he had to teach himself to juggle. He soon joined his friend and beat a hasty exit, conspicuously trying not to look conspicuous.

"We need a plan." Said Derrick.

"Absolutely." Said Eric, heading for a park-bench. Luckily, it was vacant. As they sat, Derrick said,'

"That's that new money we were reading about in the paper yesterday."

"I can see that, but is it real?" How can we tell?"

"It has to be. The real question is, why was it in the bin? That is a lot of money."

"Haven't you heard of disposable income?"

"I don't think that's quite what they mean, but on that subject, how are we going to dispose of it?"

"There's so much of it. What can you do with something that big? I don't know anyone that could take it."

"Hmm. I think I do." Said Derrick. "There's an op-shop on the other side of town."

"There's op-shops everywhere."

"True, but how many of them can change a $1000.00 bill?"

"And I thought I was the one that had lived here all his life."

"Yes. But I was a schoolteacher. Those students can teach you a thing or two. We'd better get moving, it's quite a long walk. We need to get there before they shut."

"Why don't we catch a taxi?" Eric put his hand in the bag and pulled out a note. "We've got the fare."

"Put that away!" Gasped Derrick. "I've heard of Grandma's being mugged for 50c around these parts. I can't imagine what they would do for that. No. We're going to have to leg it. Maybe if we can bum a few bucks, we can catch a bus."

"Now that's irony for you. We can afford to buy a bus and we have to beg for bus-fare."

"Ironic maybe. But not a bad idea, now I come to think of it."

"What, buy a bus?"

"No. put our trade into action." A man was walking towards them. Derrick stepped into his path and said, "Excuse me mister. Could you please spare a couple of bucks for a guy down on his luck?" The man ignored him and kept on walking. "Thanks ever so much." He turned back to Eric, "It could well be a long walk, my friend." He looked Eric up and down. "We're going to need some nice clothes as well as some day clothes too."

"Why don't we just buy some? We have the money."

"But again. We can't change the big notes without raising suspicion." Said Derrick. "I have a feeling that someone is watching for this money to come in and I don't want to be seen with it."

"Ah…," Said Eric. "I'm starting to understand."

CHAPTER 12

"I thought you said that he would definitely pay up!" Said Charlie. He thumped his hand on the table. "We waited there for over an hour. At this rate we may have to chop your finger off, and quite frankly, I don't like the sight of blood."

"I do." Said Bozo.

"I don't like the sight of mine." Said Alvin. "Something must have gone wrong. Give him a call."

"If he couldn't pay, he shoulda called. It's only good manners." Said Bozo.

"I don't recall giving him our return number, Bozo. It must have slipped my mind." Charlie picked up the phone. "I'll give him a call."

"Spooner!" Said Spooner.

"What happened to the drop off Spooner?"

"Nothing. Why? I did everything you said."

"We waited for over an hour and nothing was put in the bin bigger than a gum-wrapper."

"I put the money in the bin exactly as you said." Said Spooner. "Don't you Blank with me. There was a bin just around the corner. I pulled up, placed the brown paper parcel in the top of the bin, and left. Just as you… requested."

"Me Blank with you? Don't you Blank with me! I got a boy here who still has 10 fingers and 10 toes. I also have an accomplice who likes the sight of blood. What say we start Blanking with your son?"

"Go for it," Said Spooner. Silence fell over Charlie like all of the air had been knocked out of him.

"What?" Said Charlie confused.

"What?" Said Alvin concerned.

"What?" Said Bozo, because he thought it was a game.

"I said 'go for it'. Keep him. I don't want him back. He's cost me enough already. I'm better off without him anyway." Spooner then hung up the phone. Charlie looked at the phone as if it could give him a clue as to what just happened.

"What?" Said Alvin again.

"What?" Said Bozo. They both looked at him as you would a disruptive child.

"Well, that didn't go quite as planned."

"What do you mean?" Said Alvin. "How did it go?"

"He doesn't like you much, does he?"

"I never really made that a secret, did I?" Said Alvin. "The man is a total Blank. I don't think a whole lot of him neither. What did he say about me?"

"Nothing much. Just that he doesn't want you back. He doesn't seem to care if we chop you up into little pieces and send you in fifty different directions."

"The Blank!" Said Alvin

"Did he say anyfink about me?" Asked Bozo.

"Yeah. He said you could chop your own fingers off and shove them up your own Blank hole." Answered Charlie.

"How could I do that if I didn't have any fingers?" Charlie looked at Alvin who was shaking his head in disbelief.

"So, what are we going to do?" said Alvin.

"Hey, he's your father. You tell me." Said Charlie.

"You kidnapped me! What's your contingency plan?" Bozo was looking from one to another like he was watching a tennis match. He added,

"I know. Why don't we cut off one of his fingers and post it to him?" They both looked pointedly at Alvin.

"Wh… No! I might need them later. Look. There has to be another way."

"A toe? We could cut off one of your toes." Said Bozo, and in a lightbulb moment, "It would stop you from running away an' 'at."

"Just in case you hadn't noticed, I'm not trying to escape."

"An ear? I heard about someone cutting off an ear an' posting it."

"Would you stop trying to cut bits off of me! For Blank sake! No. We need to get him where he lives. We've got to hit him in the back pocket."

"Ok," said Charlie "we all know he's a crook and that no-one has been able to prove anything, but what can we do? What do you know that he doesn't want anyone else to know? Maybe instead of chopping you up, we could say that you gave us all this information."

"Now you're talking." Agreed Alvin, relieved that someone was trying to cut him up. "Now let me think. What are some real biggies that will cost him heaps?"

"I still reckon we should cut off his ear."

"You're not helping Bozo." Said Alvin.

"Hey." Said Charlie. "What really happened to the old mill? Was there anything done illegally?"

"Ha! Only everything! How do you think that Mr. Franko got so deeply entrenched in the old man's affairs? I bet that he's covered his tracks well enough that he can't be traced back to any of it, either."

"How can we expose this in a way that will get his attention?" asked Charlie.

"Why don't we put an ad in the paper?" Said Bozo

"Brilliant Bozo. I suppose that we could just put an ad in the paper for Spooner to give us half a Million bucks?"

"Brilliant Bozo." Said Alvin. "If we put a message in the paper that's a bit cryptic but very threatening. I think that we may just have him. And forget Five hundred thou. It just went up to a mill."

"He, he, he. That'd be a mill for a mill. He, he, he." Said Bozo

"Oh, you crack you up, don't you Bozo?" Said Charlie.

Meanwhile, on the better side of town, Sir Reginald Spooner picked up his phone and dialed. "Mr. Franko… The money has gone missing. Track it down."

CHAPTER 13

Eric and Derrick approached a small block of shops. They had decided to walk the whole way, having had the 2 busses they hailed, drive straight past them. They had stowed the paper bag in Erics' backpack for safety's sake and continued to ask strangers for money, as much for entertainment purposes than anything.

"We didn't do too bad out of that." Said Eric. "I never earned that sort of money when I was working a job."

"A very short-term income stream though Eric. People soon get tired of you asking for money all of the time. Why do you think that they don't like telecoms? We do need to hang onto it though. We'll use the big notes for this. Here we are."

"Oh wow." Said Eric. "I've driven past here a hundred times and never noticed it."

"Somehow, I don't think that that is an accident. Let's go in." Derrick opened the door and a small bell attached to a spring, tinkled.

"Can I help you gentlemen with anything?" The question came from a fairly small, older lady. The kind you just want to hug. Mostly because it would be easier to check her for weapons that way.

"Ah, my good lady." Said Derrick, taking the lead. "We are in the need of some fine clothes. Something a little cleaner and tidier than that which we are wearing. Price is not an issue."

"Price isn't an issue, eh? Are you looking for something along the same lines as 'that which you are wearing'? or maybe a business suit? Oh. And you may call me Mrs. Smith. None of this 'my good lady' rubbish." Eric took off his backpack and reached inside. Mrs. Smith, who was still behind the counter, lowered her right hand as if grabbing something from underneath. Eric removed a crisp, clean $1000 note.

"As long as you can change this, I think we may get a few different pieces." He said.

"For a small fee, I can change anything sir."

"So I've been told." Said Derrick. "And your friend still lives under the counter there, in case of trouble, I believe?"

"Of course. You can't be too careful these days. I have another, just the other side of the door as well." There was a cough from behind a curtained doorway at the back of the service desk.

"Good. We're in the right place." Said Derrick. "Let's do some shopping then. We need to look like businessmen. A nice suit each and a casual outfit should do the job, I think. Some decent shoes wouldn't go astray, either."

"That shouldn't be too hard to do." Said Mrs. Smith, eyeing the two men up and down. "You could do with a shower too, and some deodorant too, if you don't mind me saying. Pick out whatever clothes you want, and you can use the shower out the back. Toiletries are already out there."

"You are a god-send Mrs. Smith. Thank you." Said Derrick.

"It's what I do. Now, get out the back and get cleaned up." Mrs. Smith nodded in the direction of Erics moneybag. "I've got a nice bag that you might a have a use for too."

The two men selected some appropriate attire and went through to get cleaned up. Upon returning, Mrs. Smith had folded the clothes that they had chosen not to wear, and put them in a suitcase alongside a nice, neat briefcase.

"And that will be $400 even, please, on account of, I only have $600 in change." Eric handed over a $1000.00 note which she held up to the light. She rolled up her skirt, just high enough to reveal a garter with a money roll in it. She pulled out $600.

and handed it over to Eric. Holding the big note at arms-length so as to focus on the details, she said,

"I didn't expect to see one of these so soon."

"Thank you once again, Mrs. Smith." Said Derrick. "Er… Mrs. Smith? You wouldn't know of somewhere that a couple of businessmen, like us, could stay for a few nights, without attracting too much attention, by any chance?"

"Hmm… I'd say that your best bet, would be The Holiday Out, just down the road. They never check your I.D. if you don't offer, they charge by the month, week, day or hour. But don't leave any valuables in your room unattended."

"Thank you again Mrs. Smith. You are a national treasure." Said Derrick.

"Yes, thank you." Said Eric as they were exiting the door. "National treasure alright. Bet there's a few people looking for her. Did you notice that she never even asked a question?"

"Did you see the gorilla in the back room?" Asked Derrick.

"No, I didn't."

"Did you feel his presence?"

"Yes, I did."

"She didn't need to ask any questions."

"Hmm… Good point." Said Eric. "So, where to now?"

"Check in to The Holiday Out and then go on to the casino I'd say."

"What? You're going to gamble it away?" Said Eric "No wonder you live on the streets."

"No way. I've never gambled a cent in my life." Said Derrick. "No. We'll drop a couple of hundred on the tables, then change a grand or two into chips, have a few drinks… and only a few! We don't want to lose our composure. Then, cash in our chips for some smaller notes and voila! Clean money."

"Are you sure you weren't the real estate agent? Have you done this before?"

"When you're teaching kids from all walks of life… let's just say, you learn a few things yourself."

"Hmm." Said Eric. "Could be a good job that you did too."

CHAPTER 14

"Ok." Said Alvin. "So, if you call up the Willington Times and place this ad. Quote this number, it'll go on the old man's account, and we'll see what reaction we get tomorrow." Alvin started walking towards the door. "I have a couple of other calls to make to make sure this thing works properly."

"Calls like what? To who?" Asked Charlie

"I just have to make sure that all of our ducks are lined up, so we don't go off half-cocked." Alvin said. "If we aren't careful, this could all blow up in our faces."

"And how do we make sure that he delivers the money properly this time? He's had time to think about how he can get us by now. We can't have the same drop off point, can we?"

"I've been thinking about that too. I don't think that he would be expecting a complete re-run. I'll make my calls and see if it will work, or if we have to work on a plan 'B'."

"Are you sure vat we can trust him?" said Bozo, poking his thumb in Alvin's' direction.

"Bozo." Said Alvin. "If I wanted to, you would either be dead or in prison. No, you probably shouldn't trust me, but you really don't have a lot of choice."

"He really does have his old man's blood running through his veins, doesn't he?" Said Charlie.

"The difference being," said Alvin, picking up his phone, "I have a heart that pumps mine. Who knows what he has."

"So, who are you calling?"

"You probably don't want to know." Said Alvin, pressing the number into the phone and walking off for privacy.

CHAPTER 15

The next morning was as glorious as the previous one. The sun brightened the sky and the hearts of all the activewear clad trendies that were walking their pretentious pooches along the footpaths and pathways all around Willington.

Inside the Spooner mansion the curtains were drawn, and the clouds were ready to burst.

"Blank! How the Blank did they know that?" Splurted Spooner, shaking a newspaper that Mr. Franko had brought him. "Do you think that anyone will be able to work out that they are talking about me?"

"Well, by mixing up all of the initials of those words, it really did jump off the page. I do believe that it's called a Spoonerism, is it not?"

"Oh, I'm fully aware of what a Spoonerism is, Mr. Franko. But are the punters of Willington smart enough to work it out?"

"I don't think that I would be prepared to gamble on it, Sir. I think that you may have to listen to the kidnappers demands again. Besides, when we know what they are up to, we can have a little surprise waiting for them. It need only cost you the wages of a few men for an hour or two. The boys are waiting for me to let them know."

"It's nice to know that I can always rely on you Mr. Franko. You make whatever arrangements that you need, and I'll wait for the call." Franko nodded and turned to leave the room but stopped when the phone rang. "Spooner!" Said Spooner as he picked it up.

"Mr. Spooner… Have you seen today's paper?" Said Charlie. "A certain article in the classifieds?"

"Yes. I have seen it. What do you think that you're going to achieve by…"

"I think that 'we' can achieve a mutual, win-win agreement." Interrupted Charlie. "That is what I think I'm going to achieve. I have something that you want… and your son. You have something that I want, and it's gone up in value, to the tune of one million dollars."

"A million!?" Spooner boomed. "Where do you think I'm going to come up with that sort of money?"

"I would say the safe behind the picture in your office. Left 6, right 3, left 2… silly me, you know the combination. My Br… My colleague can be very persuasive." Sir Reginald was set to explode until Charlie added, "And so can his blowtorch."

"Alright, alright. Where and when?"

"My watch says 9:43 exactly. Set yours to match. Drop the money in the same bin as last arranged, corner of Long and Hall Streets, Long Street side at 12 lunch time tomorrow."

"Long Street side?" Screamed Spooner. "You didn't say Long Street side last time! Oh, Blank me!" Spooner looked up at Franko.

"Oh Blank!" Said Franko.

"It doesn't matter what was said before. Get it right this time, or we'll put the rest of the story in the papers, and I won't talk in code, if you get my meaning!" Spooner slumped back into his chair.

"I understand. 12PM. Long Street side of the corner. One million dollars." He almost choked on that last bit.

"And no tricks. We have eyes everywhere." Charlie slammed down the phone, then picked it up again and pressed the hang up button.

"Did you get that Franko?"

"Yes indeed. We have a lot more eyes than they do. I'll have the boys down there by 6AM in shifts. No-one gets past me twice."

"Let's see that this isn't the first. I want that boy back in one piece."

"I didn't know that you cared for him that much, Sir."

"I want him back in one piece so as I can take him apart myself. That little Blank gave out the combination to my safe."

"He's only a boy, Sir. I've seen some big, seasoned men, buckle under the pain of… persuasion."

"Mr. Franko. I didn't even know that he knew the combination to my safe. I want to know what else he knows. Oh, and when you do get him back, don't tell anyone that we have him, ok? These kidnappers may have become my best friends after all. Oh, and by the way, see if any of those notes have shown up yet. That sort of money doesn't just disappear."

"Er, yes Sir." Said Mr. Franko.

Charlie slid the phone across the table. "Well… That seemed to go well."

"Don't bank the cheque just yet, Charlie boy." Said Alvin, stopping the phone from sliding off the table. "He's slipperier than a snake, that Blank."

"We don't accept cheques here." Said Bozo.

"You know what I mean." Said Alvin. "Which is precisely why I had to buy some insurance."

"What kind of insurance?" said Charlie.

"It's not What you know. It's not even Who you know. It's what you know about who you know." Said Alvin. "That kind of insurance."

CHAPTER 16

"Man, that was exciting." Said Eric. "All that money flying around, and we even managed to keep ours." He was sitting on his bed in the Holiday Out, clothes and money scattered from pillow to foot. Derrick was sitting across from him on his own bed which had a nice, neat pile of folded clothes at the foot.

"Keep? I think that we even won a couple of hundred." He said, equally as excited. "That was incredible."

"And what about that waitress? She couldn't help us enough. I think that she even wanted to come home with me."

"I'm not sure if 'waitress' is her actual job description, Eric, but yes, I think that she would have loved to follow you home. A bit like a lost puppy."

"Agreed Derrick, but you have to admit, they were lovely puppies."

"May be so, my friend, but I don't think that we can afford a dog just yet." Derrick observed. "Especially one with expensive taste like that. Did you see the collar that she was wearing?"

"Yeah. Mostly for show though. They were mostly all Cubic Zirconia. If they were real, she wouldn't be hanging around a casino, waiting for losers to throw her a bone. Still, it's been a long time since a lady of any social standing has cast as much as a glance in my direction. It felt good."

"Ah yes, the real estate salesman. You would have had to pick the serious buyers from the tyre-kickers."

"Absolutely." Said Eric. "But did you hear what I said to her when she asked me how I made a living?"

"Yes. I was hoping that you were going to lie, but no. you had to tell her the truth."

"All I said was that we were in the rubbish collection, sorting and recycling business."

"And?"

"And that there was 'Big Money' in trash."

"I'm just glad that all she heard was 'Blah, blah, blah, Big Money, blah, blah."

"Yep. I don't think that she was going for the 'Thinker of the Year Award', but…"

"They were great puppies!" They both chorused and burst into laughter.

"I did think that it was funny how you got rid of that bloke that was hanging around." Said Derrick.

"Oh yeah. I was surprised that he didn't want to join our 'Multi-level Marketing business'. Such a great franchising opportunity. He looked so sharp too."

"I've never seen someone remember that he had to be somewhere else so fast in my life." Laughed Derrick. "He kept twisting his wedding ring like he was being propositioned by Puppy Girl… I dare say that he would get quite a spanking from his wife if he made any monetary decisions without getting her permission first. I'm surprised that he was allowed to go to the casino in the first place… or maybe he wasn't, ha ha."

"So, you don't think that it was the way that I was putting my arm around him then?"

"Hmmm. That may have played a part. He did keep checking to see if you'd swiped his wallet. He, he." Derrick thought for a few moments. "One thing though. At least we got to change some of those big bills into usable money.

"Yeah, that was great. We'd better get some shut eye my friend. Who knows what exciting adventures await us tomorrow."

"For starters, a warm breakfast, cooked the same day it is consumed."

"And coffee." Derrick added.

"Coffee? Oh yeah… Coffee. With maybe a splash of my special brew from tonight."

"You didn't?"

"Old habits die hard, I'm afraid." Said Eric, pulling his flask from his pocket and giving it a theatrical shake.

Derrick tipped himself sideways and put his head on the pillow and closed his eyes.

"Good night, Eric." And he fell asleep, fully dressed.

CHAPTER 17

The next morning, Eric and Derrick woke up with the sun as usual, only this time they were in comfortable and reasonably clean beds. They got up and had showers, 'like real people', as Eric put it. Although the room didn't have much, it did have a small desk built in, and on that desk was a directory with various businesses advertised in it. Neither of the men were interested in most of the tourist features, but their attention was caught by a small café just downstairs, so they made a bee-line for it. After a good feed and copious amounts of coffee, Eric said,

"Wow. I don't remember eating so well in my entire life. I have, of course, but my mind has blocked it to protect my sanity." He poured some of his flask into the coffee cup.

"More likely, you've destroyed too many brain-cells with that 'Special Brew' of yours."

"Yes, I suppose that is highly possible. They say that you should be careful what you wish for in case it comes true. I drank to forget, and now I can't remember what it was that I was trying to block out."

"Forget about that." Said Derrick. "We have much more important things on our plates."

"But we don't have any… Oh. You're being metaphorical, aren't you?"

"Yes. We need work out how to use this money, without anyone else putting claim to it… And fast."

"The casino was fun."

"Hmmm. And quite effective too. We were able to shuffle a lot more notes than I thought we would be able to."

"And who know, I may be able to catch up …."
Erics voice petered off.

"Oh no you don't!"

"What?"

"You were going to say, you might be able to catch up with Puppy Girl, weren't you?"

"No," Said Eric defensively. "Well, yes. But it was only an afterthought. Hey, you aren't jealous, are you?"

"Jealous? No. Just cautious." Derrick dropped his voice down to a whisper. "Look. We 'found' a lot of money. Someone else 'lost' a lot of money. If it were me, I'd be trying to find out where it went."

"But they threw it out. It was in the bin. They obviously didn't want it, or else they would have been a lot more careful with it."

"Even rich people don't throw money in the bin… Especially rich people. They tend to guard it very closely. No. Something has gone wrong, and we were lucky enough to be in the fall out zone. Someone will be looking for this money, and I don't want to have to explain why we have it."

"Yeah, fair enough. But who do you think would be looking for it on this side of town? After all, we're a long way from where we found it."

"I suppose so. Eh! I guess that I'm just being paranoid."

"That's right." Said Eric. "And no-one is going to be looking for a couple of businessmen. After all, we've only just gotten into town."

"Ok. Yes… You're right. So… Let's hit the casino then."

"Sounds like a plan. Let's do it."

On the other side of town, a mobile phone rang.

"Franko!" Said Franko

"Boss? Some of the money has turned up at the casino."

CHAPTER 18

Eric and Derrick were eying off the roulette wheel when Derrick said,

"That was quite a lot to change in one hit, Eric. Do you think that was wise?"

"Wisdom isn't exactly in my job description, Derrick. I'm just here to 'waste time until my next appointment'..." The last bit was said in the direction of some passers-by.

"And when is that appointment, anyway?" Just in Erics' Peripheral, he spotted Mr. Franko and an accomplice walk into the room.

"I have a funny feeling that it's been bumped forward." He said, Nodding in Franko's' direction.

"Ah craps! We'd better get out of here. I recognize the big fellow over there. He spent more time in jail than out of it since he left school. And when he was in school, he spent a lot of time 'out of it', if you know what I mean."

"Yeah, and I recognize the guy that's with him. That's Mr. Franko. He's an independent agent for the unlawful. Last I heard, he was working for Spooner. He'd be one of the few people that would have that sort of money to lose, and we don't want to get on his wrong side."

"I think that a hasty retreat might be prudent."

"I'll just cash in these chips first. Best not to act too much out of character in times like this. We don't want to attract any unwanted attention."

"Just a thought." Said Derrick. "Do you have your flask at the ready?"

"Sure, always, here." He handed it to Derrick.

"Thank you. I just wanted some insurance." He said as he poured some into his glass.

"How posh." Said Eric as he took a quick swig and put it back in his pocket.

"Change the chips then. We have an appointment, remember?"

"Huh? Oh, Yeah." Eric went up to the cashier and changed the chips back to cash. As he did, Puppy Girl entered the room, looking around to see who was there. Derrick observed a casino worker talking to Franko and pointing in their direction.

"That appointment just got really urgent, Eric. We have to fly, Now!" As Eric turned to leave, he bumped, face to face, into Puppy Girl.

"Oh, hi boys. I hoped you'd be back."

"Oh… hi… er. Um, we, er, have to leave. Sorry. I have an appointment, er, we have to go. Sorry." This was all said with Eric, half hiding, half peeking from behind Puppy Girl to see where Franko was.

"Aww. Are you not pleased to see me then?"

"I'm er, very pleased to see you, er, but the timings not too good."

"Gentlemen. Can I please have a quiet word with you?" Franko said. Derrick flung the contents of his glass into the eyes of Franko and Co. "ah, Blank, my eyes." He screamed.

"Ooh, excuse me. How careless." Said Derrick as he bolted for the door.

"Oops. Sorry. Gotta go. Bye." Said Eric as he placed Puppy Girl in front of Franko and ran after Derrick.

"Get them!" Said Franko. The thug ran after them, his eyes blurry and burning, closely followed by Franko. Puppy Girl started to follow but looked at her hands. In her left, there was her clutch bag and a mobile phone. In her right hand was a bunch of notes that Eric had passed to her. She smiled, shrugged, and slowly started dialing her phone.

CHAPTER 19

"How the Blank could they have gotten away?" Bellowed Spooner. "You had them right there!"

"I really don't know sir. We were only a few seconds behind them, but they were gone by the time we got outside." Franko rarely had to face the music, so to speak, and so he was more than a little uncomfortable.

"Now, you do have your men in place at the drop off point, yes?"

"Yes sir. Every available man is hidden around every conceivable corner. As soon as anyone goes near that bin, we have them. I wouldn't be surprised if they don't have them already." Franko nods in the direction of the paper bag that Spooner was holding. "And in the paper bag sir?"

"Just some rubbish. I didn't see any point in having a bag full of money, when they aren't going to get their hands on it."

"Very risky sir. I wouldn't want young Alvin's' life on my conscience."

"Conscience! You?" Spooner scoffed. "You don't have a conscience. That's why I hire you. And besides, what are they going to do, anyway? If they kill him, it saves me doing it, and if they try blackmailing me, I'll just deny everything. You must have done something wrong to be blackmailed. I re-read that newspaper column, and it really didn't say anything. I think that they're bluffing." As he said that, the phone rang. "Spooner!... Yes… No, and no comment. I'm not doing any interviews. And if you print anything, I'll sue you and then I'll fire you. Understand?" He slammed the phone down. "Blank!"

"What was that about?" Franko asked and then broke into a coughing fit. "Excuse me."

"It was the newspaper. They are saying that they have deciphered the message and are asking awkward questions."

"Blank me. What are you going to do? Did they say anything specific?"

"No. Just started asking me some questions about the old mill… If they can work it out, I dare say that the cops can too. You know what those journos are like, they're just as likely to get the cops to do half of their work for them."

"So, what happens when the kidnappers discover that there isn't a million bucks in the paper bag?"

"We're just going to have to stop them from opening it then, aren't we?"

As Spooner opened the door to leave, he is greeted by Charlie and Bozo, dressed as hobos. Franko reached for his gun, but Charlie already has his in his hand.

"Hello Reggie boy, and you would be Mr. Franko. I wouldn't if I were you Franko. Mines already drawn and loaded." Bozo reached in and grabbed the paper bag from Spooner and Franko's' gun. "Ah. I believe that belongs to us, now, doesn't it?"

"But…" Spooner started, but Charlies' gun being shoved in his face, cut the conversation short.

"No buts, Mr. Spooner. And don't try to follow us. You've got flat tyres." With that, Bozo grabbed the ornate door knocker and pulled the door shut.

"Blank!" Both men said together.

"I'll see if I can get their license plate." Said Franko, opening the door just in time to see several police cars, lights flashing and sirens sirening.

"Oh Blank." They said in unison. Sir Reginald put his hands up to his face and shook his head. Franko quietly slipped out the back way.

CHAPTER 20

Back at the warehouse, Charlie, Bozo and Alvin are sitting around the table with a torn-up paper bag and some pieces of ripped up newspaper, including, of course, the classified ads section.

"But I don't understand." Charlie was the first to break the silence. "I thought you said that he wouldn't Blank us 'round this time."

"Yeah. Blank us 'round this time."

"Don't worry about it." Smirked Alvin.

"Don't worry about it? I ain't doing this for the good of my health, you know. I want my cut of the cash."

"Yeah. Cut of the cash."

"Look. You said that the cops arrived just as you were leaving, right?"

"Yes. We had to dive behind the bushes."

"Yeah. Di…" Charlie pointed his finger at Bozo.

"Listen. The only reason they would go around there, all sirens and lights blazing, is if they had enough information to make something stick. They've wanted to get him for as long as forever. They won't let him go again."

"How are we supposed to get paid then?"

"I could cut off his fingers." Said Bozo.

"Let me explain this in nice simple terms." Said Alvin, turning towards Bozo. "You are not cutting off my Blanking fingers!!! Is that clear? Now. Wind back your memories a few days to when we first met. How did we meet?" Charlie and Bozo looked at each other. "Come on gentlemen. It's not a trick question."

"We kidnapped you?"

"That's right. Now, why did you kidnap me?"

"'cos your Spooners' son."

"Correct. But more accurately, I'm his only son. In fact, I'm his only living relative. If he's in the can, then I am the richest man in town. I get the lot. On paper, for taxation reasons, he made me a partner/major shareholder. At long last, his fortune can be used for good, rather than feathering his own nest." Charlie and Bozo look at him blankly, then at each other, then back at Alvin. "Sorry… Simple terms… I-will-give-you-the-money." The penny dropped and they both started nodding.

"Oh good. 'coz you was starting to worry me with all that rich talk."

"Spooner is my name, but that doesn't mean that I'm anything like him. If my old man wants something one way, I want it the other. That's the way it's always been with us. I rang Mr. Franko to set it up with him that his services would continue to be required as long as he helped nail the old man. How do you think you could walk out of there alive?”

“That’s right” Said Franko, walking up behind the brothers. “I heard you walk up to the door about 30 seconds before I opened it. The big fellow there bumped into the big potted tree by the door. I heard you swear. I had to fake a coughing fit to disguise your racket.”

“B,But I thought you was arrested” Stuttered Charlie. Mr. Franko reaches into his breast pocket and Charlie and Bozo both nearly fall off their chairs, thinking that he was drawing a gun.

“Me? Why? I have done nothing wrong. I am just a legitimate businessman. Security services. Here’s my business card if you ever need my services.”

“So… You’re not a baddie?” Said Bozo, still in shock. Alvin nodded.

"Me? Of course not. What would give you that idea? Sure, I have a bit of a reputation, but if you do the right thing by me, I'll look after you."

"Speaking of which." Said Alvin. "Did Daddy have any messages for me?"

"Ah, yes. He said, if I catch up with you, could you get in touch with his lawyer for him straight away. He wants to be bailed out ASAP."

"Oh, what a shame. I heard that they are already on the case for the prosecution. I'm going to have to call on someone else. Maybe I should call John Douhen. I hear his firm isn't overly busy."

"Not since going into partnership with Anthony Thyme. I do believe that Douhen Thyme was a bad name choice. I don't think that they've won a case yet."

"Hmmm. Might have a struggle getting bail approved then, mightn't he?"

"Hang on! How do you know who is representing the prosecution?"

"Did I ever tell you that I don't like my dad, Mr. Franko?"

"The 'Old Man' was still there when I left. They were, as they say, having a bit of a chat. I left before the coppers decided to include me in their discussion."

"Hey, they may still be there. I'd love to see him get taken away."

"You mercenary little Blank…," said Charlie. "I love it."

CHAPTER 21

"I'm really glad that we didn't burn these clothes like you suggested." Said Derrick. The two men had changed back into their original clothes. "I never thought of them as a disguise before."

"Yes. That Op-Shop was way over-priced." Agreed Eric. "I do wish that we'd laundered them though."

"Never mind. We'll get over the other side of town and blend in for a while. I kind of miss our wharf, to be honest with you."

"The bed's too hard and the alarm clock is far too unreliable, but the view can't be beaten." Eric chuckled at the irony of it all. He looked up and stopped in his tracks. "Hey, look, that's Spooner. The one I was telling you about." He pointed in the direction of the Spooner mansion, just as Spooner was being led out of the front door in handcuffs.

They must have caught up with him for lighting that big fire at the old mill. Not to mention all of the other things that he's been up to that no-one has managed to prove. Man, I bet they've been digging dirt up on him for years. Just not able to catch him in the act." Derrick was watching intently as the police carefully put Spooner into the back seat of the police car. "What's up Derrick? You've gone very quiet all of a sudden."

"I was just thinking."

"Not like you. What were you thinking about?"

"Ohh, stuff."

"Like?"

"Like, 'there but for me go I.' It's just decisions that we make, after all."

"There but for you go I, more like it. Look at the arresting officer. It's Puppy Girl in a police uniform."

"Hey, it is too. Are you sure that he's being arrested? She must be vice squad or something. Wow. Who'd have known?"

"Oooh, look. She's got handcuffs and everything."

"Stop it, Eric. We don't want you getting all thingy again, now do we!"

"I suppose not... Hey Derrick?"

"Yes?"

"I don't think that I want to re-join the real world again. I mean, this week's been fun and all, but… it's just too stressful." Derrick thought about this for a moment and said,

"You're right, you know. I don't think that I could do the whole, 'Buy a house and settle down' thing, only to spend the rest of my life, working my backside off, just to keep it. As hard as it is, I think that we may really have 'the good life,"

"I reckon that the money would change you, given enough time."

"Nah., I think you decide who you are. Money just reveals the true you, just the same as having no money has revealed who we are."

"Well, I like the you that you decided to be, my old friend. Drink?" Eric passed over the flask.

"Ahh, The Holy Grail... Why not?" He took a draught, looked at the flask, nodded, smiled, and took another. "Let's hit the wharf. Better hurry before we lose our spot. You know how valuable real estate is by the water." Derrick could feel the weight being lifted off his shoulders.

"Can we go past the 5DAY Café on the way past?"

"They're closed this time of day. They shut just after lunch... Oh, are you missing the bins?"

"No way, but there's a small fish and chip shop next door. We could share some with the seagulls."

"Great idea." The two men observed a small group of sightseers just ahead. Two of them they recognize as the pseudo-hobos from the other day, still dressed in their rags. The other, much younger one looked slightly familiar to Derrick, and had he cared to, would have realised that he was a student at the school when he taught there. They too were watching the goings-on at the Spooner Mansion.

"Here you are friend." Said Eric, handing the paper bag to Bozo, who hadn't even seen them coming. "You can use this more than me." And kept walking.

"I hope that you kept a few of those." Said Derrick.

"Of course. I may be philanthropic, but I'm not stupid."

"Whoo hooooo." They heard from behind them.

"I wonder if Puppy Girl would still be interested in coming back to my house." Said Eric.

"Why? Do you think that she might be a hobo-sexual?"

"Hey, why not? All the girls love a good bum!"

CHAPTER 22

The next morning, as the sun poked it's warm, smiling face over the horizon, a pile of smelly rags snored on the dock. A small dog gave it a wide berth, remembering the fright it got last time it got too close. A dark figure approached and perched beside the rag-pile and waited patiently. The snoring stopped, and a sole, sleepy voice drifted out.

"I so need to pee." Eric threw back the blanket to see a face staring back at him. "AHH… ohno… too late. Puppy girl?"

"Detective Jedda Bassett, actually."

"How did you find us?"

"I'm a detective. It's what I do." Said Detective Puppy Girl. "But don't worry. You aren't in trouble. I was hoping to get your help."

"You may have to speak to my friend for a minute, I, er, have something to attend to." Eric gave Derrick a rather strong nudge with his foot. "Derrick. We have company."

"Whaa?? Oh, hello… I didn't expect visitors. I'd have tidied myself up." Eric made a quiet exit to the ramp to do just that. "You have to excuse him; he has a Chinese bladder. What can we do for you Miss…?"

"Bassett." Derrick stifled a laugh. "You can call me Jedda." She frowned at him but continued. "I'm looking for these men. I'm afraid that I don't have a lot to work with, but I wondered if you may have seen them?" She handed over a security camera photograph of two men in hobo attire. One, much bigger than the other.

"hmmm. I do believe that I've seen them somewhere before. Why? What have they done?"

"Oh, we just want to see if they can help us with our enquiries in relation to an on-going investigation." Eric came sauntering back with wet trousers.

"Sorry, I lost my footing."

"Miss Bassett, here."

"Jedda." Said Jedda

"Sorry. Jedda, was wondering if we'd seen these men?" Derrick said, handing the photo over to Eric.

"Hey, that's those, what did you call them? Metro-Homeless."

"Do you know where I can find them?"

"No, not really." Said Eric "We've seen them around a bit lately, but we've never played marbles with them or anything. I don't think that they're even homeless, to be honest with you."

"What makes you say that?" He looks at Derrick who shrugs.

"I'm not really sure. Just a feeling I get. I tell you what though. Give me your number, and if I see them again, I'll let you know."

"Excellent. Here's my card. If you have any information, just give me a call, any time." She stood up. "Oh, by the way. I believe that this is yours." She handed Eric an envelope containing a wad of cash. "That was very sweet of you, but I'm not allowed to accept it. You understand."

"Thank you. I'll be in touch." Said Eric. Detective Puppy Girl left with a little look over her shoulder and a smile. "Whoa. Did that really happen?"

"I do believe so, my friend. It looks like you still have the touch."

"What do you mean?"

"Well, you wet the bed, leave the conversation to have a pee, do the laundry, come back and she gives you her number and a couple of grand. Man, I should be talking notes."

"Ha, ha. I still don't think that I could afford those puppies… Nah. I'm happy just bumming around for the time being. But who knows what the future brings. Like you said, I do have her number."

The two men packed up their kits and headed into town, because, well, that's what you do.

About Russell McKenneth

Russell McKenneth, the literary wizard from the land Down-Under calls Queensland home, where he battles kangaroos for inspiration and wrestles with plot twists while avoiding Drop-bears. Married and thriving in wedded bliss (Or at least that's what his Mrs. insists), Russell crafts tales that range from Science Fiction, to Fantasy, to Mystery Thrillers, seasoned generously with his special sauce – Humour.

Rumour has it that his writing process involves a special blend of Vegemite sandwiches and coffee strong enough to wake a snoozing Koala. So, buckle up for a rollercoaster ride through the quirky realms of McKenneth's imagination – where even Santa's Elves enjoy a good Aussie Barbie!